Happy Christmas Rowan
Lots of Love from
Uncle Ron and Aunt a   e xxx

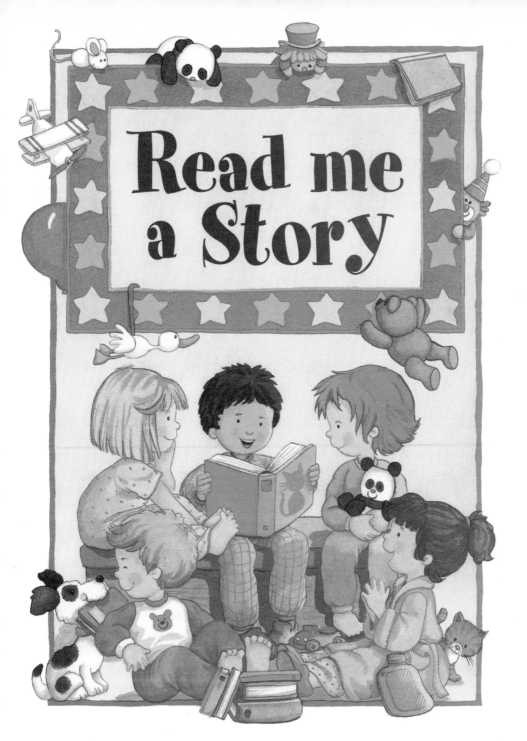

Read me a Story

Stories by Maureen Spurgeon
Illustrated by Stephen Holmes

Brown Watson
ENGLAND

First published in 2002 by Brown Watson
The Old Mill, 76 Fleckney Road,
Kibworth Beauchamp, Leicester LE8 OHG.
© 2002 Brown Watson

ISBN 0-7097-1441-6

CONTENTS

Stories by Maureen Spurgeon
Illustrated by Stephen Holmes

The Magic Carpet

Mark knew the story of Aladdin by heart! He loved hearing how he rubbed his magic lamp and how the genie granted his wishes. But, best of all, Mark liked the part about Aladdin flying swiftly across the sky on his wonderful magic carpet!

His Dad even let Mark choose an Aladdin sort of rug for his bedroom! It had stars, a moon and fluffy clouds in a deep blue sky.

'My own magic carpet!' said Mark. 'Just like Aladdin!'

Mark closed his eyes. He could almost feel himself flying through the air – until he opened his eyes and saw he was still in his own bedroom. Then, Mark remembered! Aladdin only flew on his magic carpet at night!

Mark waited until it was quite dark. Then he sat on the rug and closed his eyes tight. He felt a breeze, becoming light and warm. The rug rippled beneath him. Then he opened his eyes wide...

He was flying above towns, then over
mountains with clouds brushing against
his hair! All at once, the sky became
blue and the sun shone down on a
sandy beach.
'I wish we could land!' he cried.

Next minute, he was on the sand, palm
trees waving in the breeze! But it felt
very quiet and lonely. Mark did not like
it much. At last, he sat on his magic
carpet, wishing he knew how to make
it move.

A cloud blotted out the sun. Mark clutched at his magic carpet, trying to lift it up. Now, a whirlwind was swirling around, making Mark shut his eyes tight. 'I want to go home!' he cried. 'I want to go home!'

Mark felt himself twirling, then swirling.
Then – BUMP! Where was he now?
'Mark!' Someone was calling his name.
'Mark!' said Dad. 'I thought I heard a
bump! Did you fall out of bed!'

Mark shook his head and climbed into
bed. Flying on a magic carpet had been
exciting, but perhaps he would wait a
little while before trying it again. He
turned over and went fast asleep.

Fixit Fred

Fixit Fred loved fixing things, from a creaky gate to a broken toy! 'I'll fix it!' he said. Trouble was, Fred did not fix anything at all...

'No wonder this gate is stuck!' puffed Billy Baker. 'Fred tried fixing the wobbly handle!'

'Fred fixed a bulb in my lamp!' cried
Sally-Jane. 'Now it will not work at all!'
'And that's not all!' said Joe. 'Come
and see what Fred has been fixing at
school. You just won't believe what a
terrible job he has done!'

What a mess they found! Things were sliding off the shelves Fred had put up. There were holes in the walls where he had tried putting pictures up. Doors would not open. Drawers would not close. It was a real disaster!

'I'm off to the football match!' Fred told them. 'I'll wave at the TV cameras, so make sure you are watching!'

'Now,' said Miss Todd when Fred had gone, 'let's try mending some of the things and tidying up after Fixit Fred!'

Outside the sky grew dark and rain beat
down. 'You can all stay here until the
storm is over,' said Miss Todd. 'Switch
on the TV, Sally!'
Fred came in, soaking wet. Rain had
stopped the football match!

'Who has been fixing things?' he said.
'Look at those squiggles and dots on
the TV! I'll fix THAT!'
'No, Fred...' cried Sally. 'There is really
no need. You see the TV isn't really
bro........'

'I will fix the indoor aerial!' said Fred.
'Look! The screen is clear!'
'Sorry for the loss of the picture!' said
a voice. 'The bad storm which stopped
today's football match has also
interrupted our programme!'

'We tried to tell you!' said Sally.
'You knew I was trying to fix a TV that did not need fixing?' cried Fred. 'That is the last job I am ever doing!'
'Good!' smiled Miss Todd. 'You can play in the school football team, instead!'

'And help me train my dog!' said Billy.
'And be a clown at all the school
parties!' said Sally.
Fred had to smile! And soon he was so
busy, everyone quite forgot he had ever
been called Fixit Fred at all!

Daisy Doll

Daisy was a beautiful doll with beautiful blue eyes, beautiful hair and beautiful clothes. So it came as no surprise when the teddy bears asked her to sing at their picnic.

'I shall wear my frilly pink dress with a bow in my hair!' she cried.

Wooden Wendy was watching.
'You poor thing Wooden Wendy!' said
Daisy. 'You have nothing beautiful to
wear! Never mind! You can help me get
ready! Now, what song shall I sing to
begin with?'

'Teddy Bears Come Out To Play? Or perhaps... Sing a Song of Teddy Bears? Or what about Teddy Bear, Teddy Bear, Where Have You Been? Do you know that one, Wendy?'

Wendy looked up at Daisy.

'No,' said Wendy in a small voice.
'I shall teach you!' smiled Daisy. She
cleared her throat and began. 'Teddy
Bear, Teddy Bear, where have you
been? I've been to the park where it's
all nice and green!'

On and on, Daisy sang and sang in her high, wobbly sort of voice, over and over again. By the time she had finished, Wooden Wendy knew every, single word of every, single song! But, what a terrible noise!

'I am glad it is the Teddy Bears' Picnic tomorrow!' said Piggy Bank. 'I cannot stand much more of Daisy and her singing!' The toys agreed. But Daisy did not hear. She was already in bed, fast asleep!

Next day, Daisy was glad to see that the
sun was shining.
'What a lovely day for the picnic!' said
teddy. Then, Daisy opened her mouth
to sing – but no sound came out. After
so much singing, she had lost her voice!

'Lost her voice?' said Rabbit. 'So, who is going to sing at the picnic?'
'Why not ask Wooden Wendy!' cried Piggy Bank. 'She knows all the songs! And Fairy Doll will lend her a dress and a crown!'

Well! Wearing a pretty dress and a crown, Wendy looked beautiful!

'Do come to the picnic, Daisy,' she said. 'Voice or no voice, you can still have a lovely time with the rest of us!' And they did!

Sam and Candy

Sam the dog and Candy the cat lived in Ernie's shop. Ernie sold lots of things like nails, screws, hammers, paintbrushes and gardening tools. Sam helped Ernie to look after the shop. Candy kept busy, chasing away mice and spiders.

As soon as anyone came into the shop,
it was – 'Hello there, Sam! Good dog!'
or 'How is Sam today?' But nobody
said anything about Candy.
'I work hard, like you!' she said to Sam.
'Yet nobody notices me!'

'I am more important!' said Sam.
'Ernie needs me to chase robbers!'
'What robbers?' asked Candy. But Sam
was already running off, barking. Sue
Sharp was in the shop with her new
dog, Pickle!

'Pickle is a fine little dog!' cried Ernie.
'What do you think, Bill?'
'I think he wants me to throw him my
old wooden ruler!' said Bill. 'I have had
it since I was a boy! Can I buy a new
one just like it, Ernie?'

He held up the ruler to show Ernie. Sam barked. 'All right, Sam!' said Ernie. 'Bill is only showing me his ruler!' Sam barked again. Pickle barked back. 'All right, boy!' grinned Sue. Bill smiled, too.

Bill put down the ruler – and Pickle grabbed it in his mouth!

'No, Pickle!' cried Sue. She tried to get the ruler back. But Pickle backed away and ran off around the corner!

'My ruler!' cried Bill.

'He's squeezing under the fence!' cried
Ernie. 'Sam is too big to chase after
him now!' Just then, something brown
and furry streaked past Sam! It was
Candy, joining in the chase! She soon
squeezed under the fence!

The fur rose on her back and she hissed and snarled. Pickle barked back – and dropped Bill's ruler! He was still barking and Candy was still hissing when Ernie and Sue got there – just in time!

'Good cat, Candy!' said Ernie. He picked up the ruler. 'You made Pickle drop that ruler and got it back for Bill! What a clever cat!'

Even Sam gave a loud bark to show that he quite agreed!

The Magician

'My magic cabinet!' cried Marvo the magician. He tapped his magic wand against a tall box with a door. 'Who can I make disappear?'

'There's nobody here!' grinned Cola the Clown. 'They've all gone to the Fancy Dress Parade!'

'WE'RE here, Cola!' said Brainy
Brenda. 'Go on, YOU get inside!'
'Oh, thank you!' said Marvo. 'Now, I
close the magic cabinet. I tap the door
with my magic wand! Then, I open the
door! And...'

'Cola's gone!' gasped Brenda.
'Have no fear!' smiled Marvo. 'I close
the cabinet! I tap the door with my
magic wand! I open the door!' But the
cabinet was still empty! Cola was not
there! What were they to do?

'I bet I can find him!' said Brainy
Brenda, getting inside the cabinet.
'Shut the door, Marvo!'
'Er, I-I-I tap the door with my magic
wand...' stammered Marvo. 'Now, I
open the door, and...'

'She's gone!' cried Cheeky Chester.
'Now bring her back!'
'I-I t-tap the door with my wand,' said
Marvo. 'Then, I open the door, and..'
'Still no Brenda!' said Chester. 'What
are you going to do now?'

He began to laugh. 'This is more fun than the Fancy Dress Parade!'

'Cheeky Chester, YOU get inside!' gabbled Marvo. 'You-you'll find a lovely costume for the Parade! Go on!' He pushed Chester inside!

'It's dark in here!' came Chester's voice. 'What's more, I – aaagh!'
'Chester!' cried Marvo. He opened the door. The cabinet was empty. Then he got inside and tapped the floor with his foot...

'Aaaagh!' Marvo fell into a tunnel, swirling towards a ray of sunshine and the sound of voices. 'Marvo!' cried Brainy Brenda. 'So THERE you are!' said Cola.

'W-what?' said Marvo. 'W-where?'

'Cheeky Chester wins the Fancy Dress Parade!' came a voice, as – Marvo the Magician!'

'Well!' gasped Marvo, staring at the pointed hat and fine cloak. 'What a WONDERFUL trick!'

Make A Wish!

'I wish,' said Mandy, 'I really DO wish something nice would happen!' Mum smiled. 'So do I,' she said. Mandy's dad was in hospital and they missed him. 'What would you wish, Mandy?' said her mum. But just as Mandy started to think, the doorbell rang.

It was Mandy's friend, Lucy. She was on her new bike. Lucy let Mandy ride it around the block. The wheels whizzed around and everything seemed to flash past. Mandy was so sorry when it was all over.

'That's what I'd wish for!' she told her
mum. 'A bike of my own!'
'Well, wishing is the only way you will
get a bike!' said Mum.
'We used to wish on dandelion seeds!'
said Mum's friend, Meg.

'Dandelion seeds?' cried Mandy. 'Yes!' said Meg. 'Hold one in your hand, close your eyes, wish hard, then blow on the seed. If it floats away, you get your wish! But you must do it for three days running!'

Mandy could see lots of dandelion seeds floating in the air. It was not so easy to catch one! But, at last, she managed it. She held the seed in her hand, closed her eyes and wished very, very hard.

Then, she blew on the seed and watched it float away. 'I'll get my wish!' said Mandy. Next day, and the day after, she caught a dandelion seed. Each time, she held it in her hand, wished hard and blew!

Next day, Mandy waited for her new bike to appear. She was so sure she would get her wish! But, nothing happened. She started to lose hope. Then, the telephone rang and Mum answered it.

'Hello?' Mandy heard her say. 'Well, how WONDERFUL! Mandy will be so happy when I tell her! She's been wishing hard all week!' Then Mum gave Mandy a kiss! 'Your wish has come true!' she said.

'I – I got my wish?' said Mandy. 'Yes!'
said Mum. 'Daddy is coming home
from hospital!'

'Daddy is coming home!' Mandy
danced around, clapping her hands.
'Yes! That's what I REALLY wished!'

The Prize

'I want to win the prize for the biggest
turnip at the Garden Show!' Dad told
Beth and Joe. 'Will you help me?'
'How can we help?' asked Beth.
'I want you to water the turnip plants
each day!' said Dad.

'I grew these turnip plants from seeds!' said Dad. 'Now they are ready to plant out in the garden!'

Beth and Joe watched him putting the little plants in the earth. And next day they started their work!

First, they filled a watering can from the tap. Some water slopped onto the ground. 'Careful, Beth!' said Joe. Too late! Beth slipped on the wet patch and fell down, squashing a whole row of turnips as she fell!

Beth was not hurt. She was more
worried about the turnips! 'I saw some
more plants in the greenhouse!' said
Joe. He fetched a box of plants and
they put them into the earth, just like
Dad had done.

When Dad saw the row of new plants
and heard what happened, he laughed!
'Well,' he said, 'if your turnips grow
half as big as mine, YOU'LL win a
prize at the Show!' And off he went,
still laughing!

Beth and Joe were very excited!
'Could we win a prize?' said Beth. 'Our
turnips do look a bit small...'
'Only because we planted ours after
Dad's,' said Joe. 'Let's try and do our
best, anyway!'

All the plants grew big and strong.
Then the time came to dig up the
turnips! And what fine, big turnips
they were! Dad was very pleased!
'Your turn!' he told Beth and Joe.
'Let's see what yours are like!'

They dug carefully. 'Oh,' said Beth, 'ours are not so big and round.'
'But Dad said we could win a prize if ours were half as big as his turnips!' said Joe. 'And they are!'
'Right!' said Dad. 'Let's go!'

Well, Dad DID win the prize for the biggest turnip! Beth and Joe won a prize, too – for the biggest RADISHES! 'I was going to grow them!' said Dad. 'But now I shall leave the radish-growing to YOU!'

The Lollipop Tree

'Buy my lollipops! My lovely lollipops!
Real fruit lollipops!'
'Oh!' cried Linda. 'Can I please have a
lollipop, Mum?'
'But you have already had a banana
lollipop and an orange lollipop!' said
Mum.

'Well, can I have a strawberry one, now?' said Linda. 'Please!'

'All right!' smiled Mum. 'But this is the last one!'

'One strawberry lollipop!' said the lollipop man.

'You know,' he said, 'you should grow
your own lollipop tree!'
'A lollipop tree?' cried Linda.
'Yes!' said the lollipop man. 'Just plant
a lollipop stick in the ground and see
what happens!'

Mum laughed. But Linda licked on the
strawberry lollipop, thinking hard all
the time. Then she put the lollipop stick
in her pocket. As soon as she got
home, she ran out into the garden and
began digging.

'You are not going to plant that?' said Mum. 'The man was only joking about growing a lollipop tree!'

'I shall try, anyway!' said Linda. She put the stick into the hole and covered it over with earth.

Linda watered the spot every day, waiting to see if a lollipop tree would grow. Days went by and nothing happened. 'I told you the man was joking!' said Mum. 'Nobody can grow a lollipop tree!'

'It IS growing!' cried Linda. She pointed at the ground. 'Look! Two little leaves!' Mum was amazed. It was true. Soon, more leaves appeared, then a stalk and a stem.

'My lollipop tree!' said Linda, excited.

'No,' smiled Mum, 'it is not a lollipop tree, Linda! It is a strawberry plant! There must have been strawberry pips on the stick you planted! Those pips are seeds, and now they have grown. What a surprise!'

'That means we shall soon have lots of lovely strawberries!' cried Linda. 'All ready to make some lovely strawberry lollipops! So I did get my lollipop tree, after all!'

'Yes,' smiled Mum. 'You did!'

The Railway Coach

Tim had been given a train set on his sixth birthday. It had a signal, tracks to lay out on the floor, a red engine to pull the train, trucks for goods and one lovely, blue passenger coach. Tim liked the passenger coach best of all.

Tim liked to slide the roof off the
coach. Then he was able to reach
inside and feel the soft seats. The little
tables had a tiny lamp on them. But he
wished he had passengers to ride inside
the coach!

Time passed. Tim grew up. Now, the coach was dented and the doors were hanging off.

'What can we do with this old thing?' he asked his girlfriend. 'Do you think it is any use to anyone?'

'Put it in this box of things for the jumble sale,' said his girlfriend. 'Someone may buy it.'

'But it has no wheels!' said Tim. 'Still, I suppose you never know! Come along, we must be going!'

Tim and his girlfriend sold lots of things at the jumble sale. But nobody wanted the old passenger coach.

'You know,' said Tim, 'when I was a boy, I always wished I had some passengers to go inside!'

A lady and a girl were close by. 'No
good you hoping for a dolls' house,
Amy!' the lady was saying. 'Besides,
where could we keep it?'
Amy pointed at the coach. 'What is
that over there?' she asked.

'This?' smiled Tim. 'It is only an old passenger coach!'

'Look!' cried Amy. 'It has tables with lamps and seats which fold down to make little beds! It will make a lovely house for my dolls!'

'And we can certainly find room for it in our little home!' said Mummy.

'And I ALWAYS wanted to see passengers in that coach!' said Tim.

Amy smiled. She couldn't wait to get the coach home.

Very soon the old coach was looking almost as good as new! It still had no wheels, but Amy didn't mind. After all, with her dolls living inside, it was not going anywhere, anymore. But what a lovely home it made for them!

Rainy Day Picnic

It was the day of the school picnic. Just as the children arrived in the woods, it began to rain. 'The birds love the rain!' said Miss Hill. 'Look at them splashing about and chasing leaves across the puddles!'

That gave Suzy an idea. 'Let's race
paper boats!' she said.
They were still sailing boats and
jumping puddles, when the sun came
out again. How fresh the woods felt!
And how cool all their food was!

'A rainbow!' cried Cindy. 'Let's make a wish, quickly!'

'I LOVE rainy day picnics!' said Guy, biting into a sandwich. And, the birds? They sang and whistled as if they quite agreed with him!